MY 1ST GRAPHIC NOVEL

THE END ZONE

My First Graphic Novels are published by Stone Arch Books
151 Good Counsel Drive, P.O. Box 669
Mankato, Minnesota 56002
www.stonearchbooks.com

Library of Congress Cataloging-in-Publication Data
Mortensen, Lori, 1955-
    The end zone / by Lori Mortensen; illustrated by Mary Sullivan.
    p. cm. — (My first graphic novel)
    ISBN 978-1-4342-1289-4 (library binding)
    ISBN 978-1-4342-1408-9 (pbk.)
    1. Graphic novels. [1. Graphic novels. 2. Football—Fiction. 3. Sex role—Fiction.]
I. Sullivan, Mary, 1958- ill. II. Title.
PZ7.7.M67En 2009
741.5'973—dc22   2008031964

Summary: Olivia is fast, strong, and can catch. She loves flag football,
but the boys won't let her play. Find out if Olivia ever gets to
play flag football.

Art Director: Heather Kindseth
Graphic Designer: Hilary Wacholz

Printed in the United States of America

THE END ZONE

by Lori Mortensen

illustrated by Mary Sullivan

STONE ARCH BOOKS
www.stonearchbooks.com

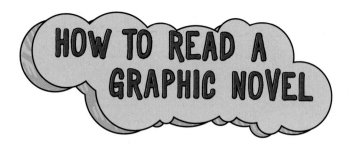

HOW TO READ A GRAPHIC NOVEL

Graphic novels are easy to read. Boxes called panels show you how to follow the story. Look at the panels from left to right and top to bottom.

Read the word boxes and word balloons from left to right as well. Don't forget the sound and action words in the pictures.

The pictures and the words work together to tell the whole story.

Olivia liked school. She liked reading. She liked writing.

6

Most of all, Olivia liked flag football.

Every day, the boys played flag football at recess. Everyone had a belt with a flag on it.

One team had red flags.
One team had blue flags.

Instead of tackling, players
would grab the flags.

The boys never let Olivia join.

They told her to jump rope instead.

Olivia didn't understand.
Boys jumped rope.

One day, Aidan was sick. The boys didn't have enough players.

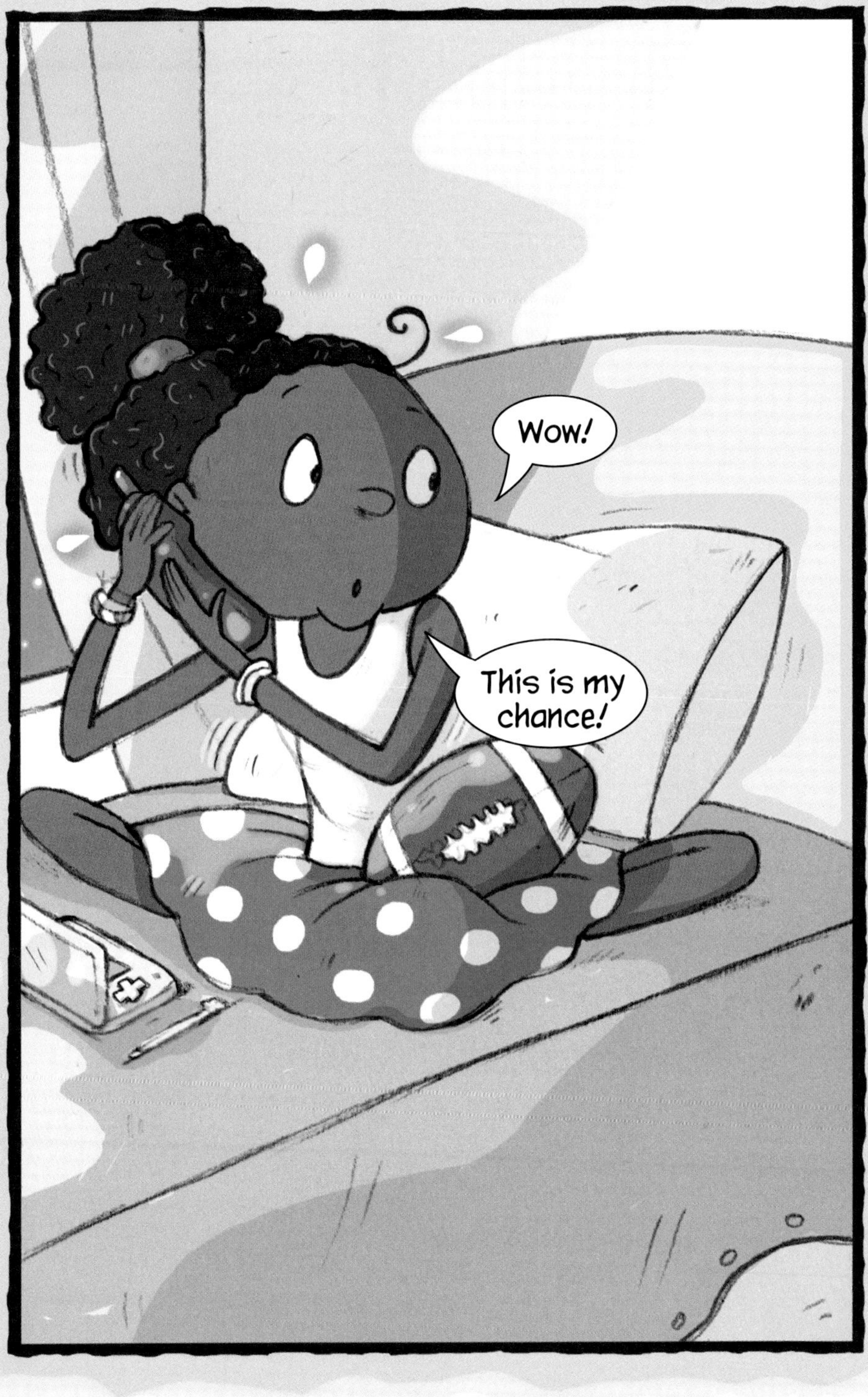
Wow!
This is my chance!

Olivia was nervous.

She was fast.

She was strong.

She could catch.

Yes!

She just had to prove it!

The next day, the red team formed a huddle.

Olivia would go out for a pass.

The red team snapped the ball.

Olivia zigged.

Olivia zagged.

Olivia reached for the ball.

Olivia missed the ball. Even worse, a boy on the blue team caught it.

WHOOSH!

I got it!

SWIPE!

Olivia grabbed his flag.

The boys on the red team were mad.

Olivia had to get the ball back.

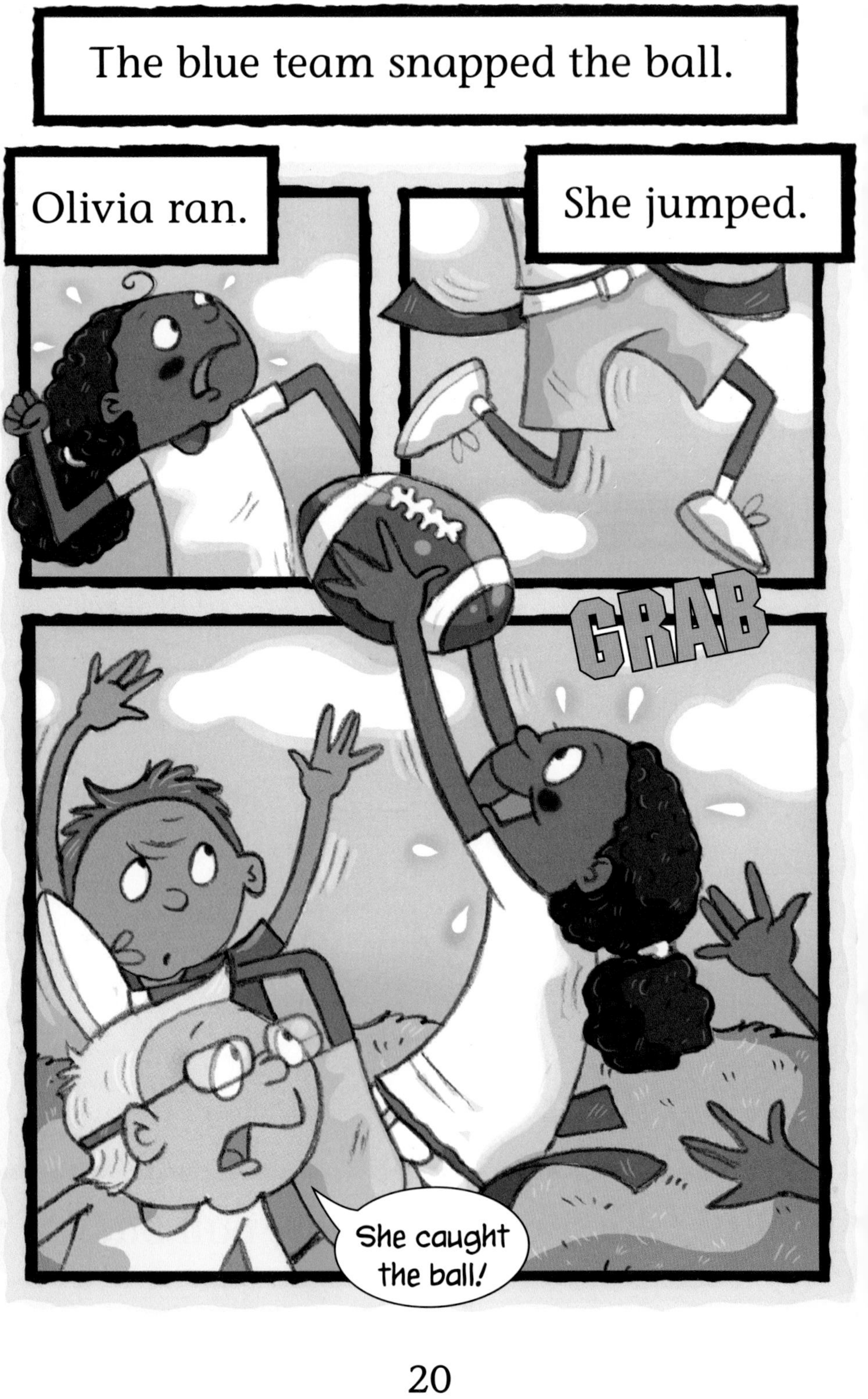
The blue team snapped the ball.
Olivia ran.
She jumped.
GRAB
She caught the ball!

She raced to the end zone. Touchdown!

The boys were happy.

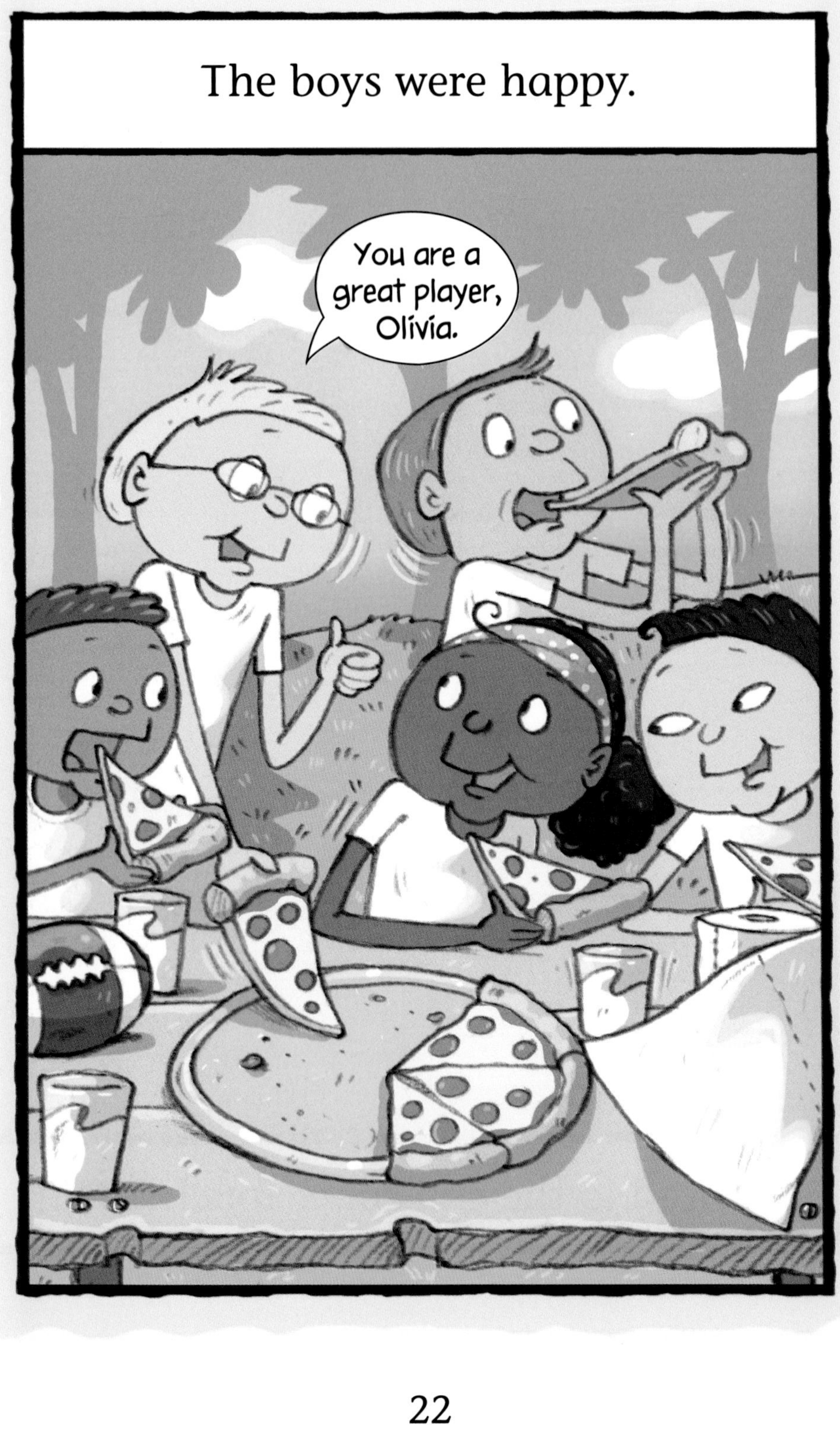
You are a great player, Olivia.

Even better, she was fun
to have on the team.

After that day, Olivia still liked reading. She still liked writing.

But best of all, Olivia loved playing flag football.

The End

ABOUT THE AUTHOR

Lori Mortensen is a multi-published children's author who writes fiction and nonfiction on all sorts of subjects. When she's not plunking away at the keyboard, she enjoys making cheesy bread rolls, gardening, and hanging out with her family at their home in northern California.

ABOUT THE ILLUSTRATOR

Mary Sullivan has been drawing and writing her whole life, which has mostly been spent in Texas. She earned a BFA from the University of Texas in Studio Art but considers herself a self-trained illustrator. Mary lives in Cedar Park, a suburb of Austin, Texas. She loves to go swimming in the lake with her dog.

GLOSSARY

end zone (end zohn)—the end of the field where a touchdown is scored

huddle (HUHD-uhl)—to gather in a group

nervous (NUR-vuhss)—not able to relax

snapped (snapt)—to put a football in play by handing it between the legs

tackling (TAK-leen)—to knock or pull a person to the ground

touchdown (TUHCH-doun)—when the other team gets into your end zone and scores six points

DISCUSSION QUESTIONS

1.) Olivia liked a lot of subjects in school. What is your favorite subject? Why?

2.) The boys wouldn't let Olivia play football with them. They weren't being fair. Have you ever been in a situation that was unfair? What was it and how was it solved?

3.) When Olivia makes an error, she doesn't get mad. Instead, she works hard to fix it. Explain a time when you made a mistake and worked hard to make it better.

WRITING PROMPTS

1.) The flag football teams are called the red and the blue teams. Write down at least three other names for each team. Then have your friends and family vote on the best ones.

2.) Olivia was good at flag football. It was her favorite sport. Draw a picture of you playing your favorite sport.

3.) Throughout the book, there are sound and action words next to some of the art. Pick at least two of those words. Then write your own sentences using those words.

THE FIRST STEP INTO GRAPHIC NOVELS

My FIRST Graphic Novel

These books are the perfect introduction to the world of safe, appealing graphic novels. Each story uses familiar topics, repeating patterns, and core vocabulary words appropriate for a beginning reader. Combine the entertaining story with comic book panels, exciting action elements, and bright colors and a safe graphic novel is born.

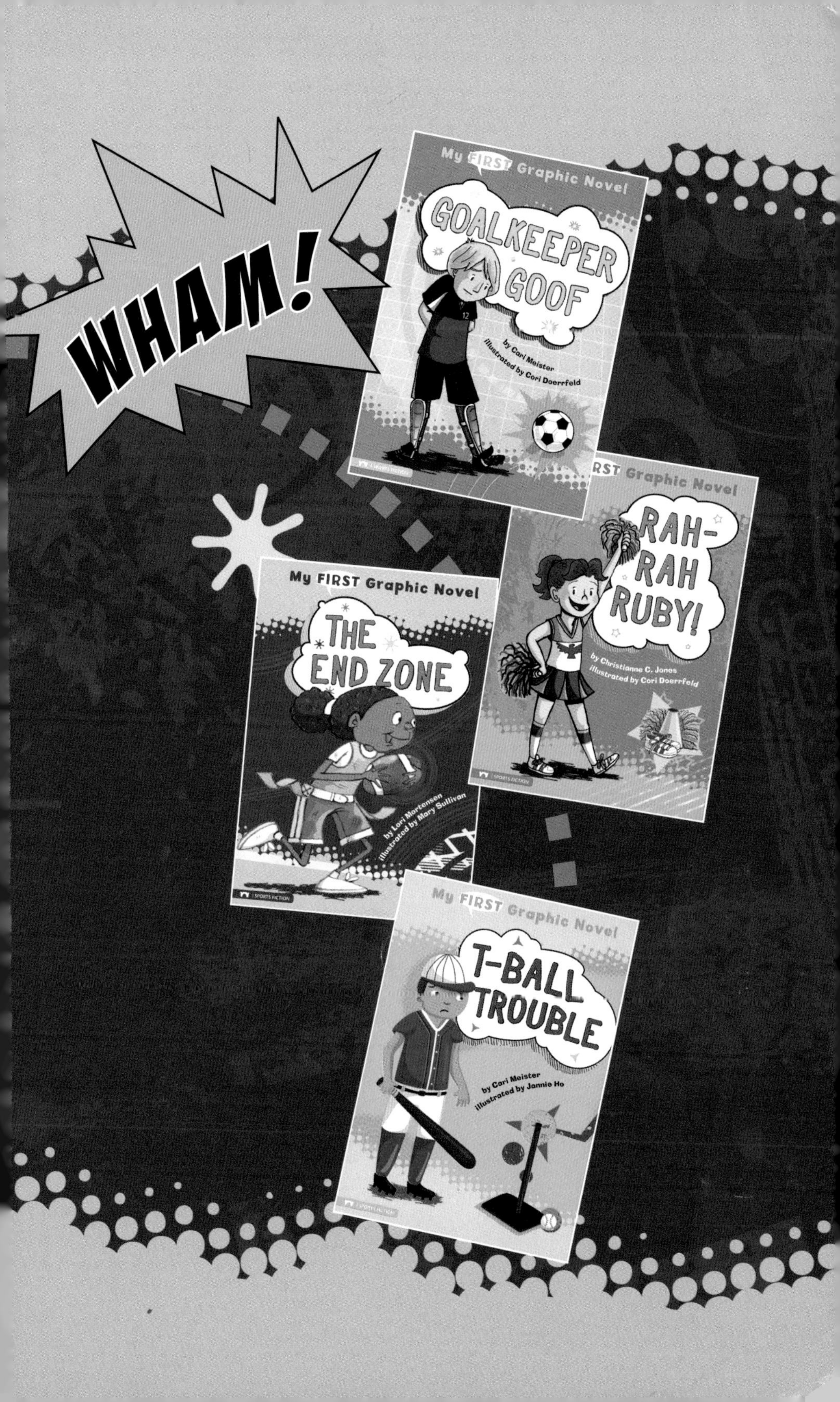
WHAM!
My FIRST Graphic Novel
GOALKEEPER GOOF
by Cari Meister
illustrated by Cori Doerrfeld
My FIRST Graphic Novel
RAH-RAH RUBY!
by Christianne C. Jones
illustrated by Cori Doerrfeld
My FIRST Graphic Novel
THE END ZONE
by Lori Mortensen
illustrated by Mary Sullivan
My FIRST Graphic Novel
T-BALL TROUBLE
by Cari Meister
illustrated by Jannie Ho